Anonymous

The Right

Hon. Benjamin Disraeli, Earl of Beaconsfield, K.G.

Anonymous

The Right
Hon. Benjamin Disraeli, Earl of Beaconsfield, K.G.

ISBN/EAN: 9783337088705

Printed in Europe, USA, Canada, Australia, Japan

Cover: Foto ©Andreas Hilbeck / pixelio.de

More available books at **www.hansebooks.com**

THE RIGHT HON.

BENJAMIN DISRAELI,

EARL OF BEACONSFIELD, K.G.,

FROM JUDY'S POINT OF VIEW,

AS SHEWN IN HER CARTOONS DURING THE LAST TEN YEARS.

RESPECTFULLY DEDICATED

TO ALL

ENGLISHMEN WHO LOVE THEIR COUNTRY,

BY

THEIR OBEDIENT AND OBLIGED SERVANT.

JUDY.

PREFACE.

SOME year and a half since we published a volume of Cartoons which might fairly be said to represent the Political History of the years 1868—78, or, at all events, that portion of it in which the Right Hon. W. E. Gladstone played a prominent part. We now supplement that volume by a second, of which Mr. Gladstone's successful Rival is the pictured hero.

The pencil of the caricaturist spares neither friend nor foe, but it is hardly necessary that the public should carry their admiration of the wisdom, foresight, and talent of the Earl of Beaconsfield to his "counterfeit presentment." To the multitude the Premier is perhaps better known by "Hyperion's curls" than either Jove's front or the eye of Mars; but it is not with the mere person of the man but with the principles he professes, with the views he holds, with the doctrines he teaches, we are concerned; and it is upon the merits of his deeds during the nearly seven years that he has held the reins of office that the nation is now called upon to pass its verdict.

For thirteen years we have steadily steered our course, never wavering; for thirteen years we have upheld those who sought to maintain the dignity of their country and the honour of their Constitution, while with pen and pencil we have shown our scorn and contempt for the rising race of pettifogging politicians, whose love of country is self-interest, and whose diplomacy is the art of shopkeeping.

Within a month England will be called upon to decide to whose charge her future welfare is to be entrusted, to either endorse the acts of Lord Beaconsfield's Government or to accept for her guides, philosophers, and friends those who, with no policy of their own and no ability to truly criticize that of their opponents, take refuge in hurling such unmeaning epithets as "Imperialism" and "Jingoism" at the Ministers who have succeeded in raising their country to her old position in the council of nations, and in proving that Englishmen have still souls above barter and ambitions above the counter.

The issue to be tried at the General Election is not of Whig v. Tory, or Conservative v. Radical, but the far higher one of Patriotism v. Peddling.

Those who love the land of their birth and rejoice to see its rulers making a stand against the pusillanimous huckstering of the jobbing cobblers of politics, will put aside all petty questions, and give their votes unhesitatingly for men who value the *prestige* of England, who honour the glory won for her by their forefathers, and are jealous of the smallest blot upon her fair fame.

With these few words we send forth our Book of Cartoons, believing firmly and sincerely in the cause we advocate, and never doubting that all true-hearted men will endorse our estimate of the political character of the Right Hon. Benjamin Disraeli, Earl of Beaconsfield.

March, 1880.

CONTENTS.

No. 1.

AN APOST.

B''les, M.A.—OUT OF MY WAY,

Mr. Beales was an agitator who, for a short time, had the confidence of the London roughs. He

OF LIBERTY.

22nd May, 1867.

OR I'LL UPSET THE LOT OF YER!

ened to destroy the Conservative Government, and succeeded in pulling down the Hyde Park railings.

No. 2.

The Conservative Government—with the late Earl of Derby as Prime Minister, and Mr. Disraeli

53

18th December, 1867.

ARTY.

ncellor of the Exchequer—received JUDY's congratulatory good wishes for the Christmas of 1867.

No. 3.

Earl of D. *(Confidential Servant).*—DON'T DRIVE TOO FAST, BEN: K
Lord Derby, on account of failing health, resigned the Premiership, and the Right

OACHMAN. *18th March, 1868.*

D.   THE IRISH MARE WILL QUIET DOWN WHEN YOU GET HER PAST THE CHURCH.

reins of Government.   The proposed Disestablishment of the Irish Church was the danger then menacing

No. 4.   22nd *April*, 1868.

NO SURRENDER.

Mr. Disraeli, on the question of the Irish Church Disestablishment, deprecated the disunion of Church and State; and, nailing his colours to the mast, fought bravely, but in vain, against the proposed disruption.

HONOUR TO

The successful termination of the Abyssinian Campaign procured for the victorious Gen

F. Proctor

HE BRAVE.

on his return the approbation of the nation, and the title of Lord Napier of Magdala.

No. 6.

"WIRED;" OR PO

W. E. G.—NOT THROUGH!!

Mr. Gladstone's Suspensory Bill having received the assent of the House of C

'ICAL CROQUET.

.L THE FAULT OF THE *LAWN*.

s, failed to pass the Lords, owing in a great measure to the votes of

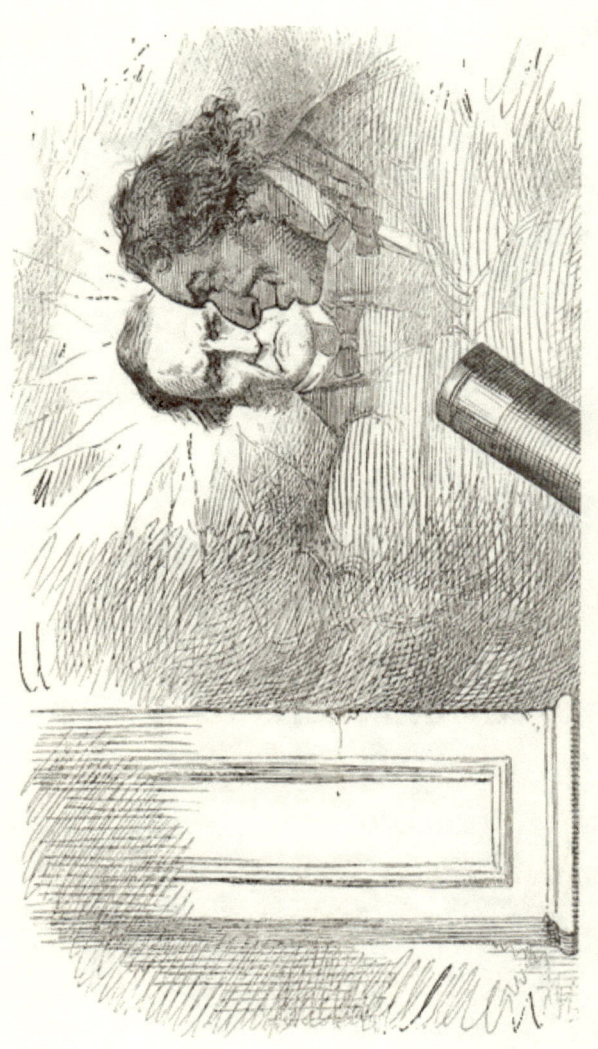

Wp. Procter

THE FIGHT FOR THE STANDARD.

(A PROPHETIC PICTURE.)

14th October,

e inevitable "Reform" combat in the next Parliament, JOHN foretold the victory of the Conservative Party.

No. 9.

AN UNPROVOKED OUTRAGE.

Low Boy.—I'LL 'AVE YER 'AT!   Second Low Boy.—I'LL 'AVE YER GAITERS!

The Liberals, in stumping the country prior to the impending General Election, did not scruple, in their desire to popularize Disestablishment, to raise a party cry against the Church and its representatives.

4th November, 1868.

No. 10.

THE YOUNG MAN OF THE PERIOD. 27th January, 1869.

Mr. Disraeli's spirited determination to uphold the union of Church and State, though it failed to gain for him a majority in the new House of Commons, increased the respect and admiration of his friends, and secured for him the complete confidence of all true Conservatives.

No. 11.

THE OLD LO[

At the close of the Session of 1869, Mr. Gladstone held a powerful majority in the House of Commo
of sound and

AND THE NEW. *18th August, 1869.*

had already sown the seeds of his own unpopularity amongst those who were not led astray by party cries ignifying nothing.

GOOD SPEED.

No. 12.

On the reassembling of Parliament in February, 1870, the Leader of the Opposition armed himself again for the fight, and once more entered the lists, cheered on by the good wishes of all those who looked upon him as the Champion of Right against Might.

16th February, 1870.

L'ALLEGRO.

The difference in the literary pursuits of Mr. Disraeli and Mr. Gladston

Hence, melancholy croaker,
Of soured hopes and evil tempers born,
Morose, grim-visaged, and forlorn !

Come hither, Mirth, thou laughter-loving joker,
" Haste thee, nymph, and bring with thee
Jests and youthful jollity !

Quips and cranks, and wanton wile
Nods and becks, and wreathed sm
These words are not original, you k
John Milton wrote them centuries a

IL PENSEROSO.

less strongly marked than their divergence of opinion on political questions.

"Hence, vain deluding joys!"
Unsuited to the William of the People,
Whose followers should weep all;

Leave merriment and jollity to boys;
Mistrust the ministers of gladness;
Hail, moody miserable sadness!

Come, gloomy sprite, and bring with thee
Morose despair and misery,
Let others with their merry laughter trouble you,
Ill-tempered gloom best suits the People's W.

AMENITIES

"Lothair," a novel by the Right Hon. B. Disraeli, was published in 1870, and achieved a rapid popularity
tendencies, made the review of this clever book the occasion of a furious and unprovoked party

LITERATURE.

hout the kingdom. Blackwood's "Edinburgh Magazine," till then known as strongly Conservative in its
: upon the Author, to the surprise and indignation of the political as well as the literary world.

No. 15.

THE SP

The growing distrust of the Government continued, and although Mr. Gladstone did his utmost to cast r
he plainly allowed his angry vexation to be seen when East Surrey

20th September, 1871.

on the possibility of any such general movement as to be worthy of the name of "Conservative Reaction," uro respectively returned Members pledged to vote with the Opposition.

No. 16.

MANCHESTER.

10th April, 1872.

On the 3rd April, 1872, Mr. Disraeli paid his famous visit to Manchester, and addressed a crowded audience in a speech which was doubtless one of the finest efforts of even his masterly elocution. All classes vied in the cordiality of their welcome to the Conservative Leader, and his visit to Cottonopolis was unquestionably one of the greatest of the many triumphs of his career.

No. 17.   QUEER CUS

Policeman John Bull *(to Superintendent Dizzy).*—THEY'RE A PRECIOUS BA

The Ballot Bill, the Alabama Claims, and the Irish Education Act occasioned considerable trouble to the Govern
                                                                                    Oppositio

MERS.

r, SIR; BUT PERHAPS YOU CAN DO SOMETHING WITH THEM.

and Mr. Gladstone professed his readiness to receive assistance in arranging these measures from the

No. 18.

A POLITICAL PAF

Mr. Gladstone's Administration having been defeated, Mr. Disraeli was called upon to form a Ministry,
with a dissolution impending, his former experience satisfied him that in attempting to discharge the r
dissolution necessary, he thought, should conclude the routine business, and then dissolve Parliament.

26th March, 1873.

E OF THE BOAT RACE.

s he declared himself able and willing to do, adding, however, words to the effect that were he then to take office
e business on hand, he would be met by factious and irritating opposition. Mr. Gladstone, who had made a

LANDLORD AND TENANT; OR, WHAT'S
THE G

Dizzy.—CERTAINLY, MR. FARMER, WE'LL DO WHAT WE C

The Landlord and Tenant Question came prominently forward, while the distr

UCE FOR THE GOOSE IS SAUCE FOR
DER.

)R YOU, BUT DON'T FORGET HODGE AND HIS FAMILY.

the agricultural labourer commanded the sympathy of all philanthropists.

No. 20.

THROWING DOW

The continually growing national dissatisfaction with Mr. Gladstone and his Ministry encouraged the
professed to look forward to it with unconcern, they yet procrastina

THE GAUNTLET.

15th October, 1873.

ervative Party to anticipate a majority in the coming general election; and though the Government
n accepting Mr. Disraeli's challenge of an appeal to the country.

JUDY'S CHRISTMAS TREE.

A PRESENT FOR A GOOD BOY.

given so many seats to the Conservatives, that even the existing Government were reluctantly compelled to acknowledge the symptoms of a reaction in public opinion in favour of the Opposition.

ELECTIONEERIN

Dizzy (to JOHN BELL).—DO YOUR DUTY, JOHN, A

As the time for the general election drew near, the Gladstone Government made most strenuous

XTRAORDINARY.   4th February, 1874.

IEY *WILL* BE "CLEARED OUT" IMMEDIATELY.

to restore confidence in themselves, and astounding bids for popularity, public favour, and votes.

THE RIVAL CUPIDS.

A POLITICAL VALENTINE.

11th *February*, 1874

The result of the elections showed, as had been anticipated, a large majority in favour of a Conservative Administration ; and, Mr. Gladstone dethroned, Mr. Disraeli soared towards the delights of office.

No. 23.

No. 24.

CAKES AND ALE; OR, THE G

Mr. Disraeli assumed the reins of Government, to the delight of all classes, every gra

D TIME COME AT LAST.

society rightly expecting to be benefited by the change of Administration.

No. 25.

Dr. Dizzy (just called in).—SUFFERING FROM LOW DIET, MR. BULL, THAT'S

The injurious tactics pursued by the late Liberal Government requir

DOCTOR.

A LITTLE BETTER TREATMENT WILL SOON SET HIM ON HIS LEGS AGAIN.

he skill of the new Conservative Ministry to remedy and counteract.

MPAIGN.   18th March, 1874.

. OF THE OPPOSITION?

irect. It became necessary for the Opposition, under these circumstances, to select a new nominal Leader
n chosen were to remain virtually under the control of the irresponsible Mr. Gladstone.

No. 27.

The Chancellor of the Exchequer.—NO, NO,

In anticipation of the Budget several deputations waited upon the

EAGER.

15th April, 1874

'AIT A LITTLE LONGER, AND YOU WILL KNOW ALL ABOUT IT.

the claims of their respective interests for the reduction of those duties and taxes in which interested.

No. 28.

BREAK

Dispersion of M.P.'s for their summer holidays at the

PROTESTANT CHURCH AND CONSTITUTION

AMENDMENTS

BILLS

G UP.

of the first Session of Mr. Disraeli's Parliament.

5th August, 1874.

No. 29.

A WELCOME THAT MIG

Mr. Disraeli projected a tour in Ireland during the autumn, b

HAVE BEEN.

reluctantly compelled to abandon the idea.

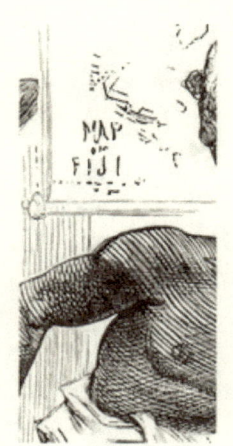

ЭT BEAUTIFUL.

) INTRODUCE TO YOU YOUR NEW SUBJECTS.

Possessions at the earnest desire of the population.

No. 31.   YOUNG SCOTLA

The growing Conservatism of educated Scotland was shown by the election of the Earl of Derby as Lord Rector c

eli as Lord Rector of Glasgow, by large majorities over their Radical opponents.

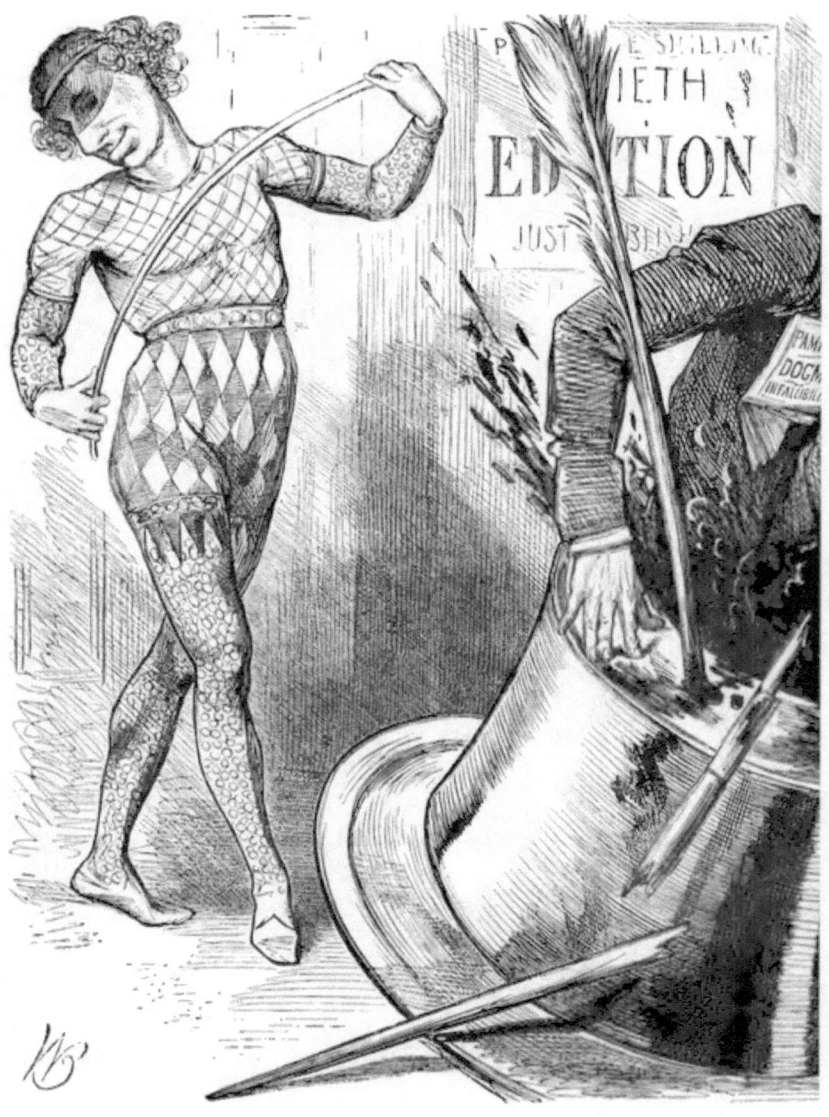

No. 32.

A BOXING-

Mr. Gladstone having devoted his leisure time to much writing on many subjects, hard
an apparently intern

JUST PUBLISHED
D GLADSTONE D
6 INCÉNSE 6

:K.

23rd December, 1874

g even those whose causes he advocated, and found himself involved in

No. 33.

UNLIMITED

Mr. Disraeli's Ministry obtained so much popularity with all classes that he was

FIDENCE.

of the energetic support of every grade of society, from the peer to the artisan

Labels on gate: SHORT NOTICE & NO LEASES / COMPENSATION / FOR IMPROVEMENTS / FARMERS GRIEVANCES / LABOUR

No. 34.

ALL THAT IS

Farmer.—IF OUR RIGHT HON. FRIEND WOULD ONLY ↑

The farmers' grievances were again

NTED.

{ THE TOP BAR, WE COULD GET OVER THE REST.

bject of legislative consideration.

No. 35.

THE PICTURE

The Right. Hon. B. D.—WELL, AS YOU DO NOT LIKE THE ACT, A
Pat.—SHURE, THIN, AND DID YOUR HONOUR IVER KNOW ME M

A large portion of the Irish Party agitated for a repeal of the Peace Preservation Act, urging

)F INNOCENCE.   3rd May, 1875.

AS I WOULD FAR RATHER YOU KEPT THE PEACE WITHOUT IT, I--- -
A DISTURBANCE?

: the action of the Government had so quieted public feeling as to render it no longer necessary.

No. 36.

At the approach of Easter the Prime Minister was able to congratulate the country on its peace, h
"financiers" had endeavoured to force upon John Bull to their ow

THE OPE

Moral.—IF YOU WANT ANYTHING "LIBERAL" DONE, 1

of admission to the Tower of London were remitted on certain days in the week:

G DAY.

EST TO APPLY TO A CONSERVATIVE MINISTRY.

: the poorer classes the opportunity of visiting the old historic building gratuitously.

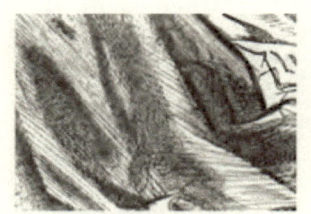

)PER WAY TO SERVE THEM.   21st April, 1875.

d on by an ex-member of the English Bar, who strove to attain popularity by appealing to the most
he lowest classes.

No. 39.

POISO

Right Hon. B. D.—WE MUST CLEAR AWAY THIS P

An abusive periodical which insulted the nation under the name of "The Englishn

S FUNGI.

28th April, 1875.

ITIAL STUFF, JOHN. IT'S A DISGRACE TO THE LAND.

i excited the disgust of all classes, far exceeded the latitude allowed to a "free press."

No. 40. THE WINNER OF THE I

Great Britain, guided by Dis

)PEAN HANDICAP.

26th May, 1875.

; the rest nowhere.

No. 41.

The Premier, secure of the approving support of the country, was impervious to the slender shafts
even the defiant threats of the Irish Home Rule

by the Opposition, more with the hope of irritating than of seriously injuring; nor could
 succeed in disturbing his equanimity.

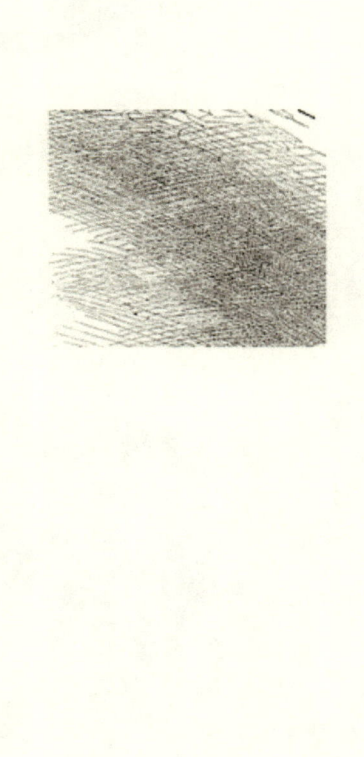

ded proprietor and the tenant cultivator, and to this end introduced the "Agricultural Holdings Bill."

No. 43.

PRINCES EAST AND WEST; OR

The Prince of Wales sailed in the " Serap

WELS *VERSUS* BROADCLOTH.

a tour through the Indian Empire.

MR BULL'S
ADVANCED CONSERVATIVE
SCHOOL.

SPEECH ON THE AGRICULTURAL HOLDINGS BILL LORD ELCHO

No. 44   A

Lord Elcho, the Parliamentary Free Lance, having with more than customary consistency

ME BOY. *28th July, 1875.*

ive Ministry, unexpectedly joined the Opposition in an attack upon the Government on the Agricultural

No. 45.

"MUCH ADO A

The Liberal newspapers combined in a snarling onslaught upon the Prime Minister and his colleagues, a
of th

T NOTHING."

11th August, 1873.

dogs baying at the moon, made a good deal of noise amongst themselves without affecting the object

THE POLIT

Dizzy.—VERY GOOD CROP, JUDY, CONSIDERING THE STORMS WE HAVE HAD

At the close of the Session the Prime Minister was able to p

18th August, 1875.

Judy.—YES, BEN. HER MAJESTY AND I ARE MUCH PLEASED.
lt of the labour of the Parliament of 1875.

MAY TH

Mr. Disraeli assisted as best

BE HAPPY!

the union of Law and Equity.

10th November, 1875.

TWO WAYS OF TREATI

THE OLD WAY.

The nation, cowed into subjection under the preceding Administration, appreciated the difference of M
opinions at the G

THE BRITISH LION.

THE NEW WAY.

17th November, 1875.

...eli's more generous open-hearted policy, and received with enthusiasm the Premier's expressed

Banquet.

No. 40.

A SEAT FOR

John Bull.—THANKS, BEN. IT'S RIGHT I SHOULD HAVE A SEAT AT THE COU

Rumours of an alliance between the Emperors of Russia, Austria, and Germany, obtained general credence,
degree exercised the minds of the alarmists. It was at this time that Mr. Disraeli, by a stroke of statesmanship,
proceeding characterized by the German press as "bold, clever, and natural."

. BULL.

ABLE WHEN THE ROAD TO INDIA IS THE SUBJECT OF DISCUSSION.

he desire of the first-named Power to push nearer the frontier of our Indian Empire had in no small
for England (by the purchase of the Khedive's shares) a preponderating voice in the Suez Canal—a

MR. BRIGHT'S PUPPET; OI

The question of a county franchise, the pet Liberal scheme for diminishing Conservative power, ag
representation, the proposal was hardly

HAT WILL THEY DO WITH HIM? *2nd February, 1876.*

upied Parliamentary attention ; but transferring as it would to the labouring class the virtual control of county
d with unqualified approval, even by the Opposition.

THE RIGH

AY TO DO IT. 9th February, 1876.

t registered the reawakened national desire for the extension and consolidation of the Empire.

WELL

Lord Lytton was appointed by Mr. Disraeli to

LITTON

PELHAM
EUGENE ARAM
LAST
BARONS, HAROLD
POMPEII, RIENZI
NIGHT AND MORNING
THE CAXTONS
LADY OF LYONS
RICHELIEU
MONEY

SYBIL
CONINGSBY
YOUNG DUKE
WORKS OF THE RIGHT HON B DISRAELI
TANCRED
LOTHAIR
VIVIAN GREY
FLEMING

)SEN.

ed Lord Northbrook as Viceroy of India·

No. 53.

UNITED ACTION OF

The Royal Titles Bill, by virtue of which Her Majesty assumed the distinction of Empress of India, met
failed to agree amongst themselves as to the ground of their hostility, the m

E OPPOSITION.

me cavilling objections from the Radical Party ; but as the various Members of the Opposition
was carried by the Government by double their normal majority.

NATIONAL
FO
PRESERVATIO

No. 54.

O.

Lord Derby (*to* Sergeant Bull).—OUR SILENT FRIEND HERE WILL KI

At the commencement of the troubles in the Balkan peninsula, Messrs. Jenkins, Kenealy,
which Mr. Disra

19th July, 1876.

E ALERT!

UT OF TROUBLE, IF POSSIBLE; BUT THERE IS NOTHING LIKE BEING READY.

d others of that class, persistently worried the Government for a formal declaration of its foreign policy,
time declined to make public.

No. 55.

NOT TO B[...]

"THE COURSE TO BE TAKEN BY A GREAT STATESMAN DEPENDS NOT UPON HIGHLY-COLOURED NEWSPAPER REP[...]

The "Daily News" and Mr. Gladstone did their best to make political ca[...]

THE
GOOD
BULGARIAN

THIS IS
LIES

AN OLD
CRIMEAN HERO
OUT OF PLACE

CAUGHT.

9th August, 1876.

OR UPON THE ACCOUNT GIVEN OF HIMSELF BY EITHER TURK OR SERVIAN, BUT UPON *ASCERTAINED FACT.*

at of sensational reports of so-called Bulgarian Atrocities—and failed.

"FINIS CO

After forty years' faithful service to his country in the Lower House, the Right Hon. Benjamin Disraeli b
manner than by showing what patience a

AT OPUS."

23rd August, 1876.

ommons to enter the Lords as Earl of Beaconsfield.   His career has benefited humanity if in no other
erance united to genius can accomplish.

No. 57.

A PERILOUS ATTEMPT.

30th August, 1876.

The Opposition, finding themselves growing daily more and more in general disfavour, in proportion as the Government gained the national approbation, made strenuous but futile efforts to obtain once more that popularity which had been formerly accorded them.

No. 58.

THE NEW YEAR'S GREETING; OR, T

Lord Beaconsfield and the Ministry received the hearty congratula

BEST OF GOOD WISHES FOR 1877.

3rd January, 1877.

the majority of the nation on entering upon another year of office.

No. 59.

Lord Beaconsfield.—THE TURK SHALL BE LOOKED AFTER,

The Government showed a wise discretion in the debates originated by the Philo-Bulgaria

7th February, 1877.

OF ENGLAND ARE OUR FIRST CONCERN.

lined to assume that attitude which Mr. Gladstone in his impetuosity

No. 60.   WELL-EARNED

At the close of the Session of 1877, Mr. W. H. Smith was elevated to the position of First Lord of the Adr
and University Members alone, not even because he was the chosen of the chief constituency in the

OMOTION.

15th August, 1877.

not to conciliate those foolish grumblers who complained that the Ministry was selected from county
ut simply because Lord Beaconsfield knew he would be the right man in the right place.

No. 61.   VERY DIFFE

The calm statesmanlike manner in which the Premier grappled with the difficulties of the Eastern
contrast to Mr. Gladstone's fierce denunciation, angry invective, and passionate verbosity, in which dipl
at Holyhead.

TREATMENT.

21st November, 1877.

ideavouring in every way to bring about a peaceful yet satisfactory settlement of affairs, was in strong
acrificed to sound and fury. *Vide* Lord Beaconsfield's Guildhall speech, and Mr. Gladstone's utterances

No. 62.   NO CHANGE

John Bull.—I LEAVE IT ALL TO YOU, GENTLEMEN, AND AM CO

In anticipation of the coming Session, the Liberals did their best to agitate the public mind again
the policy of the Earl of Bea

CESSARY. 16th *January*, 1878.

NT MY INTERESTS COULD NOT BE IN BETTER HANDS.

Government, but wholly without avail, the nation professing its complete satisfaction with ld and his Ministers.

No. 63.

ABUSE GRATIS; OR, ENVY FOL

Mr. Gladstone and other leaders of the Liberal Party, assailed the Premier in more than usuall
feelings of envy, hatred, malice, and a

ON THE HEELS OF SUCCESS.

15th May, 1878.

, betraying, unfortunately, that beneath the cloak of patriotic devotion they cherished spiteful
against the statesmen in office.

No. 64.

A NECESSARY

The victory of the Russian armies in Turkey led to the concoction of the Treaty of San Stefano, which proved t
Ministry in refusing to acknowledge the terms of Russian dictation met

RATION.

12th June, 1878.

n conditions which no English Government could suffer to pass unchallenged. The action of the
th the grudging approval of a section of the Opposition.

FANCY

DRAWN FROM THE HEATED IMAG

Premier has figured at various times, according to the views of those who have persis

THE IMMOVABLE

THE SIMPLE

3rd July, 1878.

RTRAITS.

ONS OF NEWSPAPER CORRESPONDENTS

misunderstood him, as the political harlequin, the wily diplomatist, and the simple agriculturist.

No. 66.

ALL'S WELL TH

John Bull.—THANK YOU, MY FRIENDS,

The difficulties in settling the conflicting interests of Europe were discussed at Berlin, England being repre
and the addition of Cypru

ENDS WELL.

COULD NOT HAVE DONE BETTER.

by Lord Beaconsfield in person, and the Marquis of Salisbury. The result was "Peace with honour,"

VERBOSITY

No. 67.

SPORT

Peace assu

.ND PASTIMES.

7th August, 1878.

nd Parliament prorogued.

No. 68.   DELIGHTFUL

In the trio between Austria, England, and Russia, the two foreign Powers obtained some most satisfactory

RMONY.

by closely watching the motion of the Conductor's *bâton*, and by taking their time from him.

TWO CHRISTM

The Government and the Opposition, in antagonism for the fav

HAMPERS.

24th December, 1878.

the nation, offered their Christmas presents to John Bull.

ACCEPTED A!

Mr. Gladstone, having announced his intention of retiring from the

Is it good to be fickle and fal

Is it wise to be off with the ol

THE MEMBER I

Mr. Chamberlain, the Republican, in a tirade against Lord Beaconsfield, gave utterance
"Curses, like chic

: BILLINGSGATE.

18th June 1870.

significant sentence, "Manners he has none, and his language is that of a costermonger."
ome home to roost."

No. 72.

THE USE OF A "SCI

After the taking of Cabul certain compromising letters were discovered

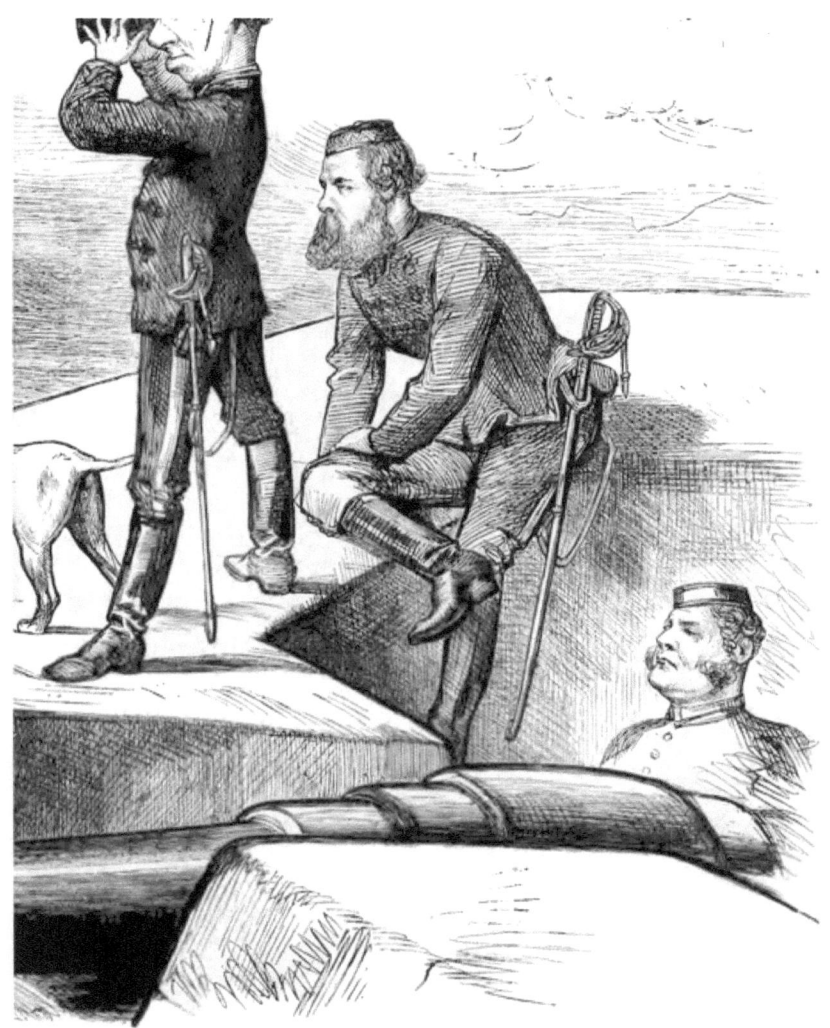

TIFIC FRONTIER."

24 S

rly proving Russia's design to threaten India from Afghanistan.

No. 73.

THE CHAMPI

On the 5th of February her Most Gracious Majesty the Queen opened Parliament in person, and the
all assailants. That at the General Election the nation will reward him for his Championship by appre
desire to see their country maintain that ascendency in the Councils of Europe which since 1873 has b

emier, for the seventh successive year as the Champion of his country, prepared to defend her rights against
g the policy of the past and looking confidently to him for that of the future, is only to say that Englishmen
the safeguard of her Honour, her Liberties, and her Trade.

www.ingramcontent.com/pod-product-compliance
Lightning Source LLC
Chambersburg PA
CBHW060602030726
47498CB00005B/1507